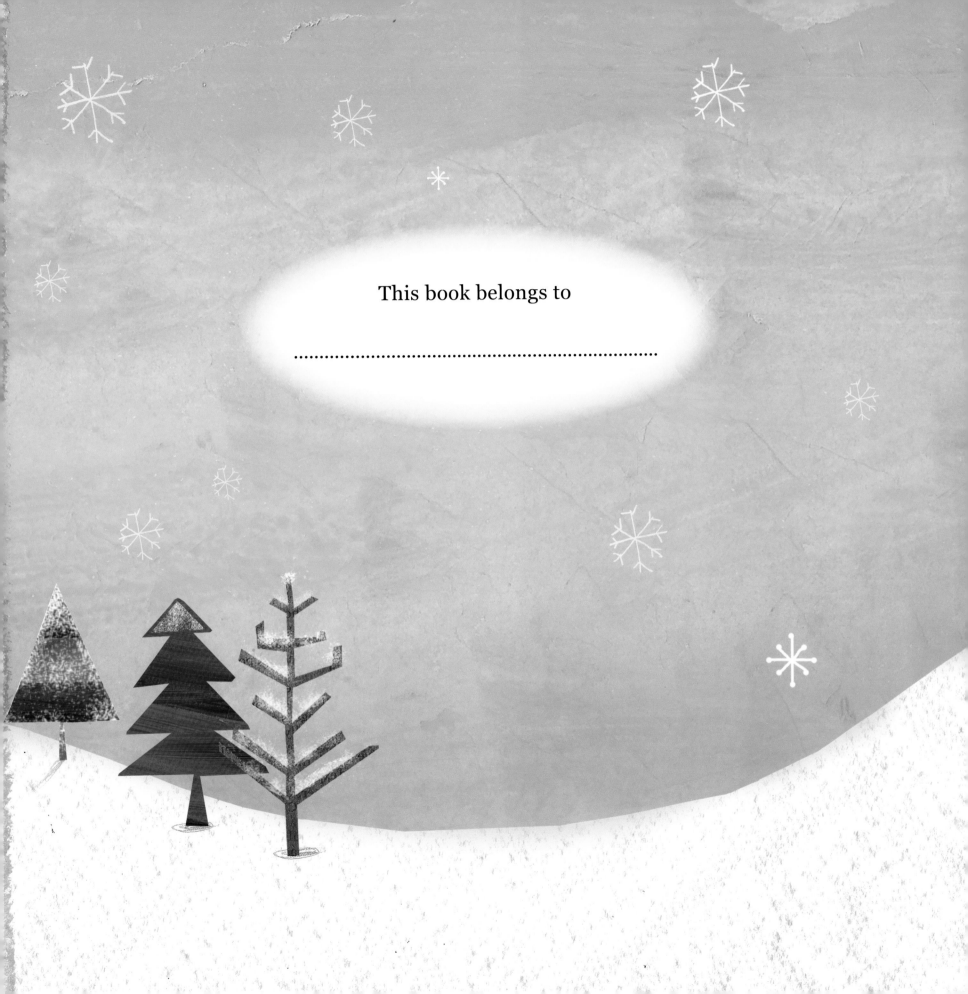

This book belongs to

....

Copyright © 2014

make believe ideas ltd

The Wilderness, Berkhamsted, Hertfordshire, HP4 2AZ, UK.
501 Nelson Place, P.O. Box 141000, Nashville, TN 37214-1000, USA.

www.makebelieveideas.com

Written by Fiona Boon.
Illustrated by Clare Fennell.
Designed by Sarah Vince.

The polar bear
who saved
Christmas

Fiona Boon · Clare Fennell

make
believe
ideas

One Christmas Eve, in a den in the snow,
a polar bear slept and so didn't know
that her cub was awake. Pip could not rest —

Z
Z
Z

he was excited for Christmas,

the day he loved best!

POLAR
BEAR
HOME

In the distance, Pip heard a jingling sound.

He jumped up and popped his head above ground.

Pressed in the snow,

he saw tracks lead away.

He said to himself,

"It must be a sleigh!"

Pip walked through the snow

'til the jingling was gone.

Alone in the cold,

he soon missed his mom.

Fresh snow hid his paw prints

and covered the tracks.

With **no** path to follow,
would he find his way back?

But then the snow stopped,

and a blaze of bright light

led Pip to a strange and magical sight.

There were warm, cozy houses
and elves everywhere –

hope lifted the heart of the cold polar bear!

Pip peered through a window as he heard a loud wail:

"Dancer's broken her leg!

Who'll take Santa's mail?"

Inside was a sleigh filled with fine toys and treats.

Nearby, an elf shouted

and stamped

his small feet.

The reindeer were worried –
they felt at a loss!
The elf looked around
and said (getting cross),

"We have seven reindeer,
but our sleigh needs eight.
If we wait for Dancer,
it will be too late!"

As they **pulled** out the **sleigh**, the elves made a fuss —
what could they do to save this Christmas?

An elf soon saw Pip and said,

"Don't be shy!

Can you pull the sleigh?"

But Pip said,

"I can't fly!"

The elves said, "Don't worry!" and put Pip in line.

"With your help,
we'll certainly
make it in time."

They **sprinkled** some sparkles and Pip gave a **sneeze!**

He felt **brave** and knew it was now **time** to leave.

Santa jumped on
and took hold of the reins.

The reindeer leapt forward,
so Pip did the same.

as the huge sleigh took flight —

The earth fell away

and Pip and the reindeer

flew off into the *night*.

They leapt across rooftops, delivering toys
to the homes of all the young girls and boys.

In bed, sound asleep,

no child was aware

that Santa's new helper

was a small polar bear!

Pip and the reindeer worked hard through the night,

delivering joy on their magical flight.

The sleigh headed home when each gift was gone.
And though Pip was tired, they all cheered him on.

Then Pip saw his den – such a wonderful sight!

He slipped from the reins and took one final flight.

POLAR
BEAR
HOME

Cozy and warm

in the snow so deep,

curled up in his bed,

Pip fell straight asleep.

Early the next morning,

no tracks could be seen.

Pip looked around –

had it all been a dream?

But in the snow lay a note
and a shiny sleigh bell,

"For the bear who saved Christmas,
Santa wishes you well."

POLAR
BEAR
HOME

For the bear
who saved
Christmas,
Santa wishes
you well